play forever on video and

Published by Ladybird Books Ltd.
A Penguin Company
Penguin Books Ltd., 80 Strand, London WC2R 0RL
Penguin Books Australia Ltd., Camberwell, Victoria, Australia
Penguin Books (NZ) Ltd., Private Bag 102902, NSMC, Auckland,
New Zealand
4 6 8 10 9 7 5
Printed in Italy

CLASSIC

Pinocchio

Ladybird

Once upon a time, there was a friendly cricket named Jiminy.

One night, Jiminy Cricket's travels took him to the workshop of Geppetto, an old wood carver.

The workshop was an amazing place. There were ticking clocks, musical boxes and wonderful wooden toys everywhere.

A little boy puppet lay on a bench. Geppetto was putting the finishing touches to him.

"Now," Geppetto said, "I have just the name for you – Pinocchio!" Then he added, softly, "If only you were a real boy…"

That evening at bedtime, Geppetto
looked out of the window. Twinkling
up in the sky was the Wishing Star.

"I wish I may, I wish I might, have
the wish I make tonight," Geppetto
said. He wished for Pinocchio to
become a *real* boy.

Soon after, Geppetto, his cat Figaro and Cleo the goldfish were fast asleep. Only Jiminy Cricket was still awake.

Suddenly, a bright blue light filled the workshop. The beautiful Blue Fairy appeared.

The Fairy looked at Geppetto while he slept. "Kind Geppetto," she said, gently. "You have given so much happiness to others. You deserve to have your wish come true."

Waving her wand over Pinocchio, she said:

> "Little puppet made of pine,
> Wake! The gift of life is thine."

Suddenly, Pinocchio began to stir.
"I can move!" he said in amazement.
"I can talk!"

"Prove yourself brave, truthful and
unselfish," said the Blue Fairy, "and
some day you will be a *real* boy."

Then the Fairy turned to Jiminy Cricket. She asked him if he would like to be Pinocchio's conscience. This would mean Jiminy would have to teach the little puppet right from wrong. Jiminy was delighted!

"Remember, Pinocchio," the Fairy said, "always let your conscience be your guide." And with that she disappeared.

Just then, Geppetto woke up and saw Pinocchio walking and talking! At first he thought he must be dreaming but then he realised his wish had come true. Geppetto was so happy he began to play a merry tune for everyone to dance to.

The next morning, a happy Geppetto sent Pinocchio off to school.

On the way, two villains, a fox called Honest John and his friend, a cat called Gideon, spotted Pinocchio skipping along.

"Look!" cried Honest John in surprise. "A puppet with no strings! We could sell him to Stromboli's Puppet Show and make *lots* of money!"

So Honest John and Gideon convinced the little puppet he shouldn't go to school. Becoming an actor would be much more fun!

Jiminy tried to stop Pinocchio leaving with the villains, but Pinocchio was too excited to listen.

That night, Pinocchio sang and
danced merrily in the puppet show.

The audience clapped and cheered
with delight. Pinocchio was a star!

However, when the little puppet
asked to go home, Stromboli, the
owner of the show, roared with
anger. "You belong to *me* now!" he
bellowed. Then he locked Pinocchio
in a cage and left him all alone and
frightened.

Later that evening, Jiminy Cricket crept into Stromboli's caravan. Jiminy tried to open the lock on Pinocchio's cage, but he couldn't.

Pinocchio began to cry. "I should have listened to you, Jiminy," he sobbed.

Suddenly, a bright light filled the room and the Blue Fairy appeared.

"Pinocchio, why didn't you go to school?" she asked.

The little puppet knew he should tell
the truth but he was afraid to.
Instead he said, "Two monsters with
green eyes tied me up and put me in
a sack!"

As soon as Pinocchio told this lie,
his nose began to grow!

The more Pinocchio lied, the longer his nose grew, until eventually there was a bird's nest on the end of it!

"Perhaps you haven't been telling the truth," said the Blue Fairy. "A lie keeps growing and growing until it's as plain as the nose on your face."

"I'll never lie again!" promised the little puppet.

So the Blue Fairy gently touched
Pinocchio's nose with her wand and
turned it back to normal. Then she
unlocked the cage and set him free.

"I'll race you home, Pinocchio!"
cried Jiminy, and off they ran.

As the little puppet raced after Jiminy he met up with Honest John and Gideon again. This time, they persuaded Pinocchio that he was ill and needed a holiday at a wonderful place called Pleasure Island.

The two villains sold Pinocchio to a
wicked coachman, who put him on
a coach full of very noisy, naughty
boys.

Luckily, Jiminy managed to climb
onto the coach just as it drove away.

Pleasure Island was like a giant fun fair. The boys could have anything they wanted and be as naughty as they liked!

Jiminy thought there was something strange about Pleasure Island and begged Pinocchio to leave. But the little puppet refused to listen to Jiminy. He wanted to stay and play pool with his new friend, Lampwick.

Finally, Jiminy gave up and decided to go home on his own.

Just as Jiminy was leaving he saw
the wicked coachman loading crates
of donkeys onto a boat. One of the
donkeys was crying and begging to
go home to his mother.

Jiminy was shocked! Somehow, all
the boys on Pleasure Island were
being turned into donkeys! Jiminy
raced off to rescue Pinocchio.

But by the time Jiminy found his friend, Pinocchio had already grown long, hairy ears and a tail!

"Come on! Quick!" cried Jiminy. "Let's get out of here."

Jiminy and Pinocchio escaped from the island by jumping into the sea and swimming home.

Cold and tired, they finally reached Geppetto's house. But there was no one there.

Pinocchio was very worried. "Maybe
something awful has happened to
Father," he said. Just at that moment,
a note floated down from the sky
and landed at Pinocchio's feet.

"It says your father went looking for
you and was swallowed by a big
whale named Monstro!" said Jiminy.
"But he's still alive at the bottom of
the sea!"

Pinocchio was determined to find
his father no matter how dangerous
it would be. He and Jiminy headed
back towards the sea.

Pinocchio tied a rock to his donkey's
tail to weigh him down. Then he and
Jiminy dived off a cliff into the water.

Down at the bottom of the sea, Pinocchio and Jiminy asked the fish and sea horses for help. But as soon as they heard Monstro's name, the sea creatures sped off in terror.

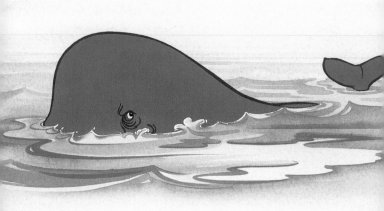

Meanwhile, not too far away,
Monstro was waking up from a long
sleep. The whale was so hungry that
he gulped down a large shoal of fish.
Without realising, he managed to
swallow Pinocchio too!

Deep inside the whale's tummy,
Geppetto, Figaro and Cleo sat in
their little fishing boat. When the fish
came gushing in Geppetto began
catching them for food.

"This one's heavy!" Geppetto cried, as he yanked a large fish out of the water. To his surprise he found Pinocchio clinging onto the fish's tail.

Pinocchio and his father were overjoyed to see each other again.

Geppetto was so pleased to see his son that he didn't mind the little puppet's donkey ears and tail.

Suddenly, Pinocchio thought of a plan
to escape. "We'll build a fire to make
lots of smoke," he said. "When the
whale sneezes, we'll get blown out
through its mouth."

Pinocchio's plan worked! As clouds of black smoke filled Monstro's tummy, he gave an *enormous* sneeze. Geppetto, Pinocchio, Cleo, Figaro and Jiminy clung to the little raft they had built as they were blown out through the whale's mouth.

The whale was furious that they had escaped. He chased after them.

"Look out!" shouted Geppetto. But it was too late! As the whale crashed through the water the little raft toppled over. Everyone was thrown into the sea and Geppetto couldn't swim!

Pinocchio managed to keep his father
afloat and drag him to the shore.

Minutes later, Jiminy found Geppetto,
Figaro and Cleo safely on the beach.
But there was no sign of Pinocchio.

The little puppet was lying face down
in the water. He wasn't moving.
Heartbroken, Geppetto took his son
home.

Geppetto knelt over Pinocchio and wept. Just then, the Blue Fairy's dazzling light filled the room once again.

"Prove yourself brave, truthful and unselfish, and some day you will be a *real* boy," said the Fairy. "You have done all of these – awake, Pinocchio, awake."

Immediately, a bright light
surrounded Pinocchio and he woke
up! He was no longer made of
wood – he was a real boy at last!

"Father, I'm alive!" Pinocchio cried
out in delight.

"This calls for a celebration!" Geppetto cried, joyfully.

Jiminy was pleased that everything had ended happily, but now it was time to move on. "Thank you," he said, looking up at the Wishing Star.

As if in reply, a shiny gold badge magically appeared on Jiminy's coat. "Official Conscience," it read. It was a reward from the Blue Fairy.

Jiminy gazed over at Pinocchio playing happily with his father. Now he knew that if you wish upon a star, your dreams really can come true!

Yours
to own
on DISNEP
DVD

WALT DISNEP
CLASSICS

Magical stories to